STARRY NIGHT

Also by Orion Taraban

The Value of Others:
How to Get (and Keep) More of What You Want
in the Sexual Marketplace

STARRY NIGHT

ORION TARABAN

ISBN: 979-8-9900695-3-4 (Audiobook)
ISBN: 979-8-9900695-7-2 (Paperback)
ISBN: 979-8-99-00695-8-9 (Ebook)

Editing/Proofing: Jennifer Jas
Cover design: Tracy Kimball Smith
Ebook/Paperback formatting: Tracy Kimball Smith
Audiobook engineering: Bruce Abbot

Cover photograph: Agriesti, H. *Verso of Two Poplars in the Alpilles near Saint-Rémy*
[Photograph]. The Cleveland Museum of Art.
Back cover paintings:　Van Gogh, V. (1890). *Portrait of Dr. Gachet* [Oil on canvas].
Private Collection.
Van Gogh, V. (1889). *Self-portrait with bandaged ear*
[Oil on canvas]. The Courtauld Gallery, London.
Van Gogh, V. (c. 1887). *Portrait of Theo van Gogh/Self-Portrait*
[Painting]. Van Gogh Museum, Amsterdam.

For Vincent

This book is a novel inspired by real events.
Though it largely accords with the facts as we know them,
the story remains – ultimately – a work of fiction.

CONTENTS

EVENING

The voices had returned. Like the objects of a familiar room taking shape in the early hours of morning, they seemed to materialise out of an expectant nothingness. At first, it was difficult to tell whether they had actually come back or whether he was merely recalling a memory – the exhausted echo of an incident best forgotten. However, the impressions lingered. They would not be silenced by work or wine, coming even to limn his dreams with a dreadful hue. Until finally, like the long-awaited appearance of the sun, they crystallised into a hideous certainty and insisted upon their recognition.

All day, he contended with the voices. He had long since learnt the mocking ones – always female – could be deflected with a sad acquiescence. After all, what defence could he possibly mount against them? His failures were never far from him. Rather than argue, his rebuttal was a melancholy silence, a small nod, and a slight smile.

The accusing ones, on the other hand, were not satisfied by this display of appeasement. They penetrated deep into his soul with a perverse tenacity. In haughty and overfamiliar tones, the voices spoke of his emptiness, his worthlessness, his sin. Like a butcher hacking at the joints of a carcass, they dismantled his thought – the pretence of self, the impossibility of meaning – until it was reduced to a confused welter, screaming in incoherence.

Against the accusers, nothing could be done. Their attacks were brutal and insistent and relentless – and any reaction on his part only seemed to goad them to further viciousness. All that remained for him was to withstand the onslaught: to become a thing, insensate and unmoving.

However, he was wrapped in a body he could not make unfeeling, and the voices were inexhaustible.

Their return marked the onset of an agonising attrition. Like an outnumbered contingent in desperate retreat, he would surrender scraps of his soul – his reason, his dignity, his memory – to slow their advance. However, the conclusion of his flight was foregone. While the sun was shining – while the created world was still clear and distinct – he could fasten his mind unto the fixed forms of reality. This was the bulwark on which he could lean when his limbs were sapped of their strength. But night would soon arrive, and there would be nothing left to protect him from its seething profusion. He would need to act before he lost the will to do so.

Staggering through the streets that led out of the village, he gripped the fabric of his trousers so his unsteady steps would not jostle the revolver from his pocket. A storm was approaching. The tall spires of the cypress were already shaking in the wind, and a flock of crows, roused from their nests, circled ominously overhead. As he progressed along the path, the thatched-roof houses scattered about the fringes of the town gradually gave way to sprawling tracts of wheat, heavy with the prospect of harvest.

Halting on a small rise, he let out a gasp. Filtered through the disturbed atmosphere, the sunset was arrayed in an uncommon magnificence. The empty sky was burnished a brilliant gold, while the clouds that menaced the horizon hid a crimson stain. Like coins in a stream, the first few stars already sparkled through the watery firmament. And beneath it all, the stalks of wheat danced in murmurating unison, as if fingered by the hand of a sportive god. The voices grew silent. The beauty of the scene – the vibrant colours, the tasteful composition – wrenched his heart with a pang of uncomprehending awe.

The boundary fell away. No longer standing before the world like an artist before a canvas, he had been pushed through the frame, thrust into the painting. He was light and form and arching line. He could feel the texture of the sky and sense the movement in the fertile soil. In such moments – when the self is sloughed like a skin outgrown – his life was bearable and his existence redeemed. Was this the only way?

But the world would not keep still, and the landscape – like a febrile patient on a physician's table – was bled of its vitality. Darkness stole across the sky. Advancing clouds obscured the infant stars and smothered the gibbous moon. The fields dissolved into the uncertain distance, feeding a void that writhed with the coming squall. The ecstatic union of evening had become the creeping terror of night. Deprived of sight, the mind perceived what vision could not – the wind had eyes, the trees had teeth! – and he felt small and afraid.

This would not be the first time the darkness had devoured him. What preserved him was not hope or strength, but the body's stubborn refusal to die. Should night overtake him, his body would survive again. But the man housed within – the body's cryptic cargo – had grown tired and frail. If a container once shattered does not quite return to form, then what of a vessel repeatedly dashed? Would its contents not leak through the ill-fitting pieces? To what pitiful ends could a man deprived of sense be applied?

He drew the gun from his pocket and cocked the hammer. The darkness was close – very close. He could feel its breath upon his trembling face. He gripped the barrel with his left hand and pressed the muzzle into his chest. The winds swirled around him as the voices rose in a jangling chorus of laughter. He gasped as the inky substance of the night began to pour into his nose, his mouth. In helpless censure, he raised his eyes to the heavens, but nothing met his gaze.

As he tensed his hand, lightning streaked across the sky in a brilliant flash. A muted crack and the smell of brimstone. The sudden, irrepressible urge to lie down. A country garden. His father's back. The swimming earth. And the unexpected recollection that one has forgotten that one has forgotten.

On the evening of July 27th, 1890, Vincent van Gogh, aiming for his heart, shot himself with a revolver.

He missed.

THEO

Though the day was still young, the railway carriage was already uncomfortably warm. Sunlight blazed through the row of windows on the right-hand side as the train crawled through the northern suburbs of Paris. Like the other men in the compartment, Theo was dressed in a three-piece suit. As his body rocked in time with the train's undulations, he could feel the perspiration start to form on the nape of his neck. Soon it would be streaming down his back. Instinctively, he began to remove his tweed jacket. However, an image of the other passengers eyeing his shirt sleeves with judgemental glances flitted across his mind, and he resigned himself to the heat.

The message had arrived at dawn. Like all telegrams, it was very short. But the note nevertheless succeeded in evoking in him an inchoate dread. Apparently, Vincent had suffered some kind of accident and Theo's presence was urgently requested in Auvers-sur-Oise. No further details were included. So after hastily packing a case and informing his wife of his business, he hurried to catch the next train departing from the Gare du Nord.

As he watched the countryside move across his field of vision, Theo worked through the various scenarios he might encounter when he arrived. What kind of accident could have befallen his brother? Perhaps he had tumbled off a rooftop or proven too "careless" with his razor. If the injury were serious, then surely the telegram would have mentioned it. But if it were of little consequence, then why was he needed "urgently"? Why send a wire at all?

No, the accident must have been grievous, though he could scarcely imagine what to expect. To inoculate himself against the shock he sensed forthcoming, he attempted to conjure various disturbing images in his mind's eye: his brother's mutilated face, a cold and rigid corpse. He pictured himself brave and stoic and useful in the midst of the tragedy, but this only incited in him a vague self-pity. Should he truly be entertaining such awful thoughts, in any case? Perhaps it fell to him to remain faithfully committed to the positive. As the train swayed in its forward progress, so too did his mind vacillate between fear and hope.

He let out a small sigh. There was little point in guessing what awaited him in the village. He would know soon enough. Relaxing his gaze, he noticed his reflection in the windowpane. A copse of oak, some passersby, a shard of sky: each briefly filled the spectral outline of his image floating in the middle distance. We become the sum of what life passes through us, he mused.

Though four years Vincent's junior, Theo was often mistaken for the older brother. However, their outward similarities belied characters of striking contrast. It was as if all the traits with which a single man could be endowed had been portioned between them: where the one excelled, the other was bereft. Viticulturists maintain that variance in soil and clime produces wine's extraordinary diversity. What then could account for such disparity between two fruits of the selfsame vine?

Since Vincent was indisposed to worry after his own well-being, it fell to Theo to do so on his brother's behalf. Though he would occasionally enjoy periods of clarity and relative stability that could last for months at a time, Vincent never long refrained from giving his brother cause for concern. Indeed, the intervals between lapses had been shortening of late, and the violence of his episodes had grown considerably stronger. And after the Christmas incident, Theo was finally dispossessed of any remaining illusions with respect to his brother's madness. So when Vincent announced his desire to quit the asylum two months ago, Theo was filled with grave misgivings.

"I'm not sure I understand." The air in the room grew thin, and Theo's heart began to beat heavily in his chest. "You want to leave the hospital?"

Sitting in a chair by the cell's only window, Vincent did not meet his gaze. Staring through the glass, his eyes were fixed on something his brother could not see.

"But you've been doing so well. These last few months in particular. I feel as though you've made great strides." He paused. "Are you not happy here?"

Vincent cast him a sharp look before returning to the window.

"That is to say, don't you think your time here has not been entirely unpleasant?"

"My Theo, that is precisely the issue." Vincent looked down at his hands. "I want what is best for me. You want only that I should not suffer the worst."

"Not an unreasonable aim, given the circumstances," Theo muttered in his self-defence.

"It is unreasonable. To save a life, it must be worth the saving. What reason could there be in preserving such an existence?"

Theo shuffled his feet. Though he hadn't expected this turn of events, he was well acquainted with his brother's obstinacy. "What is it you want?"

"To paint."

"To paint?" Theo laughed in disbelief. "Then what, may I ask, have you been doing with yourself this past year? You've done nothing but paint!" He gestured to the rows of canvases stacked against the walls, three or four pieces deep, all turned away. "Honestly, I've sometimes wondered whether your painting left you enough time for your treatment. In any case, your tenure here has hardly impeded your productivity."

"Those are not paintings. I cannot paint here."

"What do you mean, they are 'not paintings'?" He picked up a canvas, turned it around, and placed it on the easel, which – along with the stiff-backed chair on which Vincent sat and the iron-frame bed in the corner – constituted the room's only furniture. "Then what do you call this?"

Upon seeing the image on the canvas's face, Theo's first reaction was to regret his own gambit. The piece was striking, yes – but strange. It seemed to depict the view from the cell's window – he could recognise the lanky cypress and the softly undulating hills – but a small town had been planted in place of the surrounding fields, and other details appeared embellished.

However, it was the night sky above the village that commanded his attention. Moist and refulgent, it looked as if the element itself were being warped, coiling into massive whorls of air. A spattering of stars capped the scene with their shimmering coronas. The overall effect was pleasant enough, but the vibrant colours would be too intense for patrons who were wont to associate impressionist paintings with pastels. It would be a difficult piece to sell. At least it was small.

Vincent glanced over to see which painting his brother had taken up. When he recognised it, his mouth twisted into a slight grimace. "I call it what you would if you were honest. A failure."

"'Failure' is a bit harsh," Theo replied. He then turned back to the easel and made a show of looking at the piece more carefully. The paint had been applied in thick ridges with a palette knife, creating the unsettling illusion the night was seeping off the canvas. "It looks like you've been working with impasto." He turned toward Vincent with a smile. "Taking risks is demanded of the avant-garde. In any case, it's not bad for a study."

"You know it was not meant as such," Vincent returned. "My days of study – such as they were – are behind me. Today cannot merely be a preparation for an uncertain tomorrow." He looked around the room. "These abortions accuse me. They are the miscarriages of a disordered womb. I cannot bear to look at them."

"You must be patient, brother. The season we sow is not the season we reap. What you seek is already inside of you. It needs only the time to emerge."

"And if I'm only afforded a season?"

"You cannot know that," Theo spoke with more forcefulness than he intended. "To live in the shadow of death is to live as a man condemned." He shook his head. "It is not good to dwell on such things. It will hinder your recovery. Better to remain here until the cure has taken hold. I know it won't be long."

"It has already been a year. If water could soothe my distemper, it would have done so by now."

"It is not the baths," Theo rebutted, "but the peace and calm, the simplicity of an ordered life, that heals."

"Voices are heard most clearly in a quiet room," Vincent replied, turning back to the window.

Theo attempted to conceal his panic. "You didn't tell me the voices had returned. What do the doctors say? How long has this been going on?"

The wind rustled the leaves of the oak in the courtyard. Vincent considered the tree's trembling limbs for a time before responding.

"I remember when I last went mad. It was only when you came to me in Arles that I understood what I had done. Your eyes were full of terror, full of pity. I saw then a part of me – a part I hadn't noticed – lived in you. And in doing violence to my head, I had managed to wound your heart. I could not bear to look at you, but you would not leave my side.

"I have come to this place – and lived a year within its walls – because of those eyes. In the empty hours of the night, I see them still. They speak what your mouth cannot. That I am an intolerable burden. That I am a source of pain from which your love will not permit you to escape. I know you would never abandon me. You are too maddeningly good for that. So I spared you the shame of a betrayal: my gift to you. I left Paris while I still had the strength, before I could destroy us both.

"Here in Saint-Rémy, I hoped to release you from the embarrassment of my presence. No lurid headlines, no rumoured half-truths. If confining myself to this room could absolve you of your bond, I would remain here for the rest of my days. And when the powers on high came to judge the merit of my life, I would put forth my resignation as the greatest of my works."

Theo shifted his weight uneasily.

"But it has done no such thing," Vincent continued. "Quitting Paris could not remove me from your thoughts. How could it? You are reminded every month to send the money required for my upkeep." He looked at his brother and winced. "What kind of man cannot earn the bread that sustains him? You have a son at home – an infant – and a wife. And yet you squander the funds that ought to be devoted to their care on misplaced hopes and useless cures. Johanna must despise me."

"You know she harbours no resentment for you."

"I know she would never admit it," Vincent rejoined. "Perhaps not even to herself. It would impugn her Protestant decency. And you are not so different." He looked down at the ground. "The love that motivates your charity is tainted with loathing: each cheque is ransom paid to escape the guilt you would otherwise feel."

"I wish you would not speak this way," Theo mumbled.

"And I wish I could unsee what I have seen," Vincent replied. "But I am full of sight, cursed with sight. I see what others would if they did not pretend to see, which is what clouds their eyes." He smiled faintly. "You are more worldly than I, brother. But I can tell you the blind have no use for one who sees. His vision is an offence to their darkness."

Theo rubbed the back of his neck. "No one has yet seen the world as you do. Your vision is startling, unsettling. People clamour for novelty, but they are frightened when it appears. Your paintings are like stepping out of a dark room into the blinding light. You must allow time for the public's eyes to adjust."

"And how much time do their eyes require? They have already been adjusting for ten years! Do they need twenty? Forty?" He shook his head. "No, it is not more time your public requires. They have had opportunity enough, and they have rendered their verdict with their silence."

"One day, your name will be included among the great masters. I am convinced."

"I am less so," Vincent said with a small frown. "In any case, if such a day comes, I will not be here to see it. It is the envy of others – not the tastes of the public – that hinders my recognition. To celebrate one's peer is an affront to one's dignity.

"Dead artists are easier to love than living ones," Vincent continued. "If I am ever respected, it will be as an idea – not as a man. But what good is respect to an idea? It is the living who demand – who require – our consideration, our admiration, our respect. Ideas have no use for such things."

Theo gave a small shrug. "To achieve success, the idea must precede the man. It is the idea that teaches people how to see, what to feel. It is what transforms a mere painting into art. You know this."

"I am not interested in success," Vincent replied ruefully. "I do not paint for money or for fame. I paint because I cannot refrain from doing so. I paint because I will otherwise be destroyed. The act of painting is as needful to me as breath. It is what delays my dissolution and binds the world together. My work might be your business, but to me it is neither a pastime nor a vocation: it is survival."

Theo moved toward his brother. "I know. I know, Vincent. That is why I think it best you remain in the hospital. Here, the banal concerns of life cannot find you. You need not traffic in the sordid compromises of the marketplace or suffer the city's constant indignities. You can rest and paint and ensure your survival."

Vincent's eyes flashed. "Do you still not understand? That is why I must leave! I cannot paint here! The forced leisure, the professional sympathy: they bind me as tightly as any straitjacket. I am stiff, stifled; I cannot move as the work demands. And yet the vision burns brightly within me. It sears my mind's eye. If I could produce what my mind conceives – if I could deliver it whole onto the canvas – then I might survive the ordeal and be done with it.

"But it will not issue! Like a child who refuses to be born on an inauspicious day, the creation remains buried inside of me, restless and wriggling." Beads of sweat began to form on his brow. "Bed rest will not relieve this discomfort. The work must be extracted. And so I labour day and night to effect its birth – to expel it while it lives – but all that emerges are flakes and fragments. My mind is clenched around its frame and will not let it go!"

Vincent began to tremble. "My condition is dire. If I cannot rid myself of this passion – if I cannot realise what my stubborn heart insists I can create – then the visions will languish inside me. They will suffocate, and they will die." He clenched his fists. "Do not misunderstand. I would not grieve them. They have stolen more from me than you will ever know.

"But these stillborn creatures would soon begin to rot and decay. Like the corruption that spreads from a gangrenous limb, the blight would seep into the blood, the organs. It would not take long for the springs of life to spoil, and – like a thwarted mother whose bed becomes her bier – I would follow my breathless children into death.

"This is why I must leave this place." He turned back toward the window. "I cannot paint here."

Theo stared at the back of his brother's head, feeling the stirrings of his impatience. He understood he would need to proceed with care.

"I would like to help you, Vincent. You tell me you cannot paint here. But please understand: right now, we do not know if you can paint elsewhere. As distasteful as these walls might seem, they may not be responsible for your troubles. The difficulties of which you speak," he softened his voice, "they arise from within. You cannot forsake them so easily. Like your own conscience, they will follow where you go."

"It is of little consequence," Vincent responded.

Theo's eyes widened. "This is no small matter! How would you fare without the hospital? How would you eat? Where would you sleep? If you were to leave, I cannot guarantee your well-being."

"I am not well, Theo. I have not been for some time, and I may never be again." His eyes brimmed with intensity. "I understand your concerns. I may die if I leave the hospital. However, I tell you – with absolute certainty – I will die if I don't. And I see little reason in renouncing a lesser risk for a greater one."

Theo could sense he was losing ground. "You worry me."

"Exactly!" Vincent exulted, moving toward his brother. "My time here was designed to ease your cares, but they continue unabated. If anything, the unseeing distance has distorted them further. My commitment has not brought you the peace either one of us had intended."

"While you suffer, what peace exists for me?" Theo replied.

"My God," Vincent sneered, "you would be less cruel if you were more unkind. Your goodness wounds. It shames! I cannot feel but small and angry in its shadow."

Theo looked at him uncomprehendingly. "What would you have me do?"

Vincent drew up close, his eyes flashing. "I would that you were honest with me! Where is your frustration? Your rancor? Your disgust? After so much disappointment and despair, would you still pretend to perfect benevolence? A mountain stream is not as pure as your unsullied heart."

Theo looked at him in silence. Years of chaos and uncertainty were etched in the lines of his face, but what use would there be in objecting? The contagion must not spread. He would not sink to the level of Vincent's temptation. Like a firebreak that starves the blaze for want of wood, he arranged his features into an indifferent mask, devoid of emotion. "I will not argue with you, brother."

Vincent continued to glare at Theo. For a small eternity, the brothers faced each other, tense and unmoving. Vincent's eyes bored into Theo's impassive expression, provoking him to react. Theo imagined they had both been preserved in some unearthly resin, suspended in time.

Somewhere in the distance, a bell began to sound, measuring out the remnants of the morning. One after another, the muted peals broke upon the room like an implacable tide, washing over the unmoving men, only to ebb once more into silence.

As the final toll faded away, the tension began to drain from Vincent's body. He took in a deep, jagged breath and relaxed his hands. Slowly, he shambled back to his chair by the window and settled into its seat with exaggerated care. His eyes looked tired and confused, like a subject who had just broken free of a hypnotist's spell. After a few moments of dawning comprehension, a light tremor crept into his body, and he began to cry.

Theo watched his brother's breathless shuddering floresce into gasping convulsions. As Vincent's moans filled the room, Theo released his own strain in a noiseless sigh. His brother's quivering figure excited no pity in him, nor did his lack of response arouse any self-recrimination. All he could sense was a profound exhaustion that seemed to surround him like a featureless landscape.

Theo observed his own body move across the room to place a hand on his brother's shaking back. This was the gesture the present moment demanded. The next would call for a different response, and the one after that, another still. And all these moments were linked in an inexorable chain of obligation that stretched unto the ever-receding horizon. Theo did not know how much longer he would need to walk this path, but he was growing increasingly concerned that God had given him enough strength to do so.

Vincent's ragged breathing gradually settled into a rhythm, his anguished cries yielding to stifled sobs. When he lifted his head to look at his brother, beaded tears still clung to his eyelashes. Meeting Theo's gaze, he managed to eke out a sheepish smile, his eyes dark and sorrowful. He looked like a lost child just reunited with his mother – relieved to be home, but uncertain as to whether he would be punished for running away.

Theo squeezed his brother's shoulder and spoke in the most reassuring tone he could muster. "The more violent the storm, the more quickly it passes." He gave Vincent an understanding smile and turned to survey the room. "Are you hungry?"

Vincent looked blankly at his brother.

"I daresay I could eat," Theo declared. "It's a bit early, but I imagine someone will be able to accommodate us. There isn't much a hot meal and a little rest can't put to rights. Why don't you lie down while I go in search of a nurse?" And before waiting for his brother's response, Theo slipped out of the room and closed the door behind him.

The hallway was cool and empty. In the privacy of the darkened corridor, Theo pressed his back against the lime-washed wall and allowed himself the luxury of a few deep breaths. If he waited long enough, Vincent – drained from this morning's events – would be asleep by the time he returned. This would afford him the opportunity to make a tactical retreat without having neglected any of his fraternal duties. Tomorrow, he might be able to make some headway with a more equilibrated Vincent. Forbidding him to leave would be futile. However, he might still be able to influence his course through mild perseverance.

As his eyes acclimated to the lack of light, subtle forms began to emerge from the darkness: irregularities in the texture of the wall, variegation in the shadows. Scraps of speech – made indistinct by their gentle caroming – wafted in from adjacent wings of the hospital. Ensconced in this liminal world, Theo sank into a deep reverie.

Like a sliver of ice in a pool of sunlight, he could feel himself sublimating into the gloom. He melted into the wall against which he leaned. He became the wall, had always been the wall: a wall endowed with sight and devoid of judgement. He was the hallway's silent, secret witness. Without purpose, he fulfilled it. Without action, he left nothing undone. And with an indifference that knows no alternative, he would watch this dimly lit passage until passage and pillar collapse into ruin, and ruin itself is undone by the merciful erosion of time.

A door opened further down the corridor, pouring a fan of golden light onto the floor. Jolted out of his phantasy, Theo stood up straight and prepared to greet whoever would appear – but no one came. Like a man awaiting the arrival of a long-delayed train, he continued to look in the direction of the light in dwindling anticipation. Eventually convinced of his solitude, but no longer feeling alone, Theo grew progressively embarrassed by his own presence. He didn't know how long he had been standing there, but he was sure it had been long enough for Vincent to nod off. He pressed his ear to the door of his brother's cell and held his breath. He could sense no movement in the room beyond. Feeling reassured, he opened the door and stepped inside.

He found Vincent awake in his chair, just as he had left him.

Theo felt his stomach drop. A vision of the next several hours – difficult and pointless – flashed in his mind.

He suppressed the sudden urge to leave the room, leave the hospital, flee Saint-Rémy, and take the next train – not to Paris (there was death in Paris, and his wife's anxious eyes), but to a place he did not know and so could not be followed – to a different country, where there were no asylums or paintings or brothers, and no one spoke to him for any reason whatsoever since he could not understand the language.

Vincent had not yet acknowledged Theo's reappearance. He continued to stare into the emptiness before him, his focus piercing through the walls. Suddenly, Theo recalled his deception and reproached himself for returning empty-handed. His wishful thinking hadn't prepared him for this possibility. "I couldn't find a nurse," he offered lamely by way of explanation.

Vincent turned in the direction of his voice. When his eyes alighted on his brother's face, his brows contracted slightly, as if he were struggling to recall a dream. The sunlight angling through the window pooled in Vincent's lap, illuminating his hands with uncommon brilliance.

"Have you ever watched a day pass away?" Vincent asked.

Theo understood this to be a question, but there was no inflection in Vincent's voice, which sounded as though it were travelling across a great distance. "I've seen many sunsets," Theo replied.

Vincent frowned in response. "People imbue sunsets with undue significance. A sunset is merely the day's last breath. The day does not die at dusk: it has been dying all along. While the sun is high, there is life enough to contend with death – so it's hard to hear the groaning of the day. But those plaintive sighs are always present for those who would listen. Yet there are few who do. Why is that?"

Theo was unsure how much longer he could stay in this room. "Because the world will not wait. Those deaf to your rumblings have their ears full with the sounds of life. They hear their duties and responsibilities. There is little time to contemplate the night while the day's work remains undone."

Vincent scoffed. "People mistake urgency for importance. They are ashamed to admit their 'work' amounts to very little. It is busyness for the sake of busyness. If their activity possesses any significance, it is precisely this: that it might distract – for just a while longer – from the night's contemplation. This is its chief function.

"For who could hear the groans of the day with a heart unmoved? These are sounds that wrench the soul from its complacency and – once heeded – cannot be unheard. They awaken a man to his real responsibilities: to forgive, to repent, and – having repented – to love. And to love what? Not a corpse or a concept – they are easy enough to love – but his fellow man: with all his texture and shadow and incomprehensible symbolism. And his fellow man needs love. More than he knows, and more than he deserves.

"So people plug their ears and drown out the sighs. Too much of the day yet remains, and that is a long time left to love. People want to love – but not much, not yet. Like schoolchildren, they put off the lesson that would further their education as long as possible. It is only at the end of the day – when the sun sinks low on the horizon – that their task becomes bearable, for they know it will be over soon. They watch the sunset like those who attend the final moments of a neglected relation: with the guilty relief they did not come earlier."

"Not all are as callous as you would have them be," Theo replied.

"True," Vincent conceded, "most are far worse. They are willfully committed to their deafness. And this is why my work – despite your faith and efforts – will never be accepted. Every one of my paintings – irrespective of its theme – bears witness to the day's passing. And this is exactly what people make a determined effort to ignore. They attend to the light only when it starts to fade, because at this point they may be absolved for doing so little."

Theo remained silent for some time. "I think you should remain here in the hospital."

"I have already discharged myself," Vincent confessed, turning back to the window. "I am simply waiting for you to leave."

It was mid-morning when the train pulled into the station at Auvers-sur-Oise. The promise of a hot summer day had been fulfilled. As he briskly walked through the cobbled streets, Theo felt increasingly abstracted. The contrast between the gravity of his errand and the nonchalance of the village created a sense of being out of place, out of time. Peddlers hawked their wares. Women gossiped in the storefronts. If death resided here, then it could be presumed he was on holiday.

In a few minutes, he was standing before an unassuming inn whose name he recognised from his brother's letters. Having come all this way, he was seized by an intense reluctance to go inside. He had gotten there very quickly. Surely, no one would be expecting him yet. Perhaps he could find a secluded corner in some empty café or stroll along the river's embankments. Whatever misfortune had befallen his brother could not now be prevented. What difference could his presence possibly make?

The advance of an oncoming coach jostled him out of his inertia. Tense and resigned, he approached the inn's front door and stepped inside. The first floor was comprised of a small restaurant. A dozen small, wooden tables were spread out over an open floor of black-and-white checked tile, while a small bar with well-stocked shelves lay vacant to one side. Two men sat at a table, discussing market prices over coffee. Unsure of what to do, Theo stood in the doorway, awkward and unacknowledged.

As he scanned the room with mounting unease, he detected the figure of a young girl crouching behind the banister of a staircase near the rear of the hall. Perceiving she had been discovered, the girl slowly stood and stared at Theo with a searching expression. He returned her gaze impassively. Seemingly emboldened by his observation, the girl crossed the parlour with a queer sense of purpose, as if sent on an errand to fetch an ingredient whose name she could not pronounce.

"Mr. Theo?" she asked tentatively.

Theo startled slightly, surprised to hear his own name. "Yes?"

As if overtaken by a sudden diffidence, the girl looked down at her hands and picked nervously at the front of her frock. "Mr. Vincent is in his room upstairs," she mumbled to her shoes.

Theo looked back at the staircase. Her task complete, the girl did not wait for a response. Skirting around Theo, she slipped out the front door and disappeared into the street. Exhaling deeply, Theo walked across the restaurant and started up the stairs.

As he ascended, the room at the top of the landing came into view. The door was ajar. Through its opening, Theo could see an older man with a narrow face sitting motionless in a chair. There was a wistful, languid manner about him, as if he only moved with great reluctance. Stirring from his study, he rose to intercept Theo before he could enter the room.

"Theo, I presume? Thank you for coming." The man extended a hand with a sombre air. "I am Doctor Paul Gachet. I have had the honor to call your brother a friend since he arrived in Auvers."

Grasping the outstretched hand, Theo glanced over the doctor's shoulder into the room beyond. He could see a pair of legs tenting up a cotton bedsheet. Unmoving and akimbo, the legs looked frail and thing-like beneath the tautly stretched cover. The chamber seemed very quiet.

Theo looked back at Gachet, his head beginning to swim. His limp hand slid out of the doctor's handshake. "What has happened?" he asked in a hoarse whisper.

Gachet inhaled sharply. "We don't have all the details, but it seems as though your brother was involved in some kind of firearms accident."

Theo stared blankly. "Firearms?" He might as well have told him Vincent had just been recovered from the wreckage of a Chinese junk in the Sargasso Sea. "How can that be?"

"You will have to ask him yourself," Gachet responded, his eyes darting to the side. "The innkeeper summoned me as soon as Vincent returned with his injury, and I have attended him ever since.

"His condition is stable, but altogether critical. It is clear he was shot in the chest, but I could not find an exit wound. Most likely, the bullet ricocheted off his rib and lodged itself in his abdomen. His stomach – and possibly his spleen – have been punctured. I have done my best to stop the bleeding." Gachet drew up close and dropped his voice. "However, the bullet is inaccessible. I'm afraid it is only a matter of time."

Theo felt faint. His eyes flitted back and forth between the doctor's face and the covered legs. Though he hadn't foreseen a gunshot, this was one of the scenarios he had prepared himself to meet on the train. Or, rather, it was a possibility he had been half-expecting for years. It was only the fact it had occurred today of all days that could possibly be considered surprising. And yet, for all his covert speculation and morbid rehearsal, Theo found himself completely unprepared for the actual event. He certainly did not feel sanguine and resolute. At that moment, all he could sense was a kind of relief at having finally been liberated from an anxious anticipation.

"Is he in pain?" Theo asked.

"Not currently, but I daresay he was suffering a good deal when I found him." Gachet smoothed his moustache with an index finger. "Gut wounds are excruciating, by all accounts. That he was able to walk himself back from the scene of the accident is – quite frankly – incredible. I gave him another draught of laudanum no more than an hour ago. He should be resting comfortably."

When he finished speaking, Gachet remained looking at Theo with the eagerness of a boy who – having spent half the night studying – was impatient to demonstrate his knowledge. However, realising no new questions were forthcoming, he continued with a note of disappointment. "Vincent is a man of uncommon virtue. The world is brighter for his having been in it." He placed a reassuring hand on Theo's shoulder. "You should be proud to have him for a brother."

Theo looked into Gachet's face. The doctor's paternal gesture – combined with an awareness of his own helplessness – elicited a felt sense of dependence on the physician. He inwardly rankled at the ease with which this was accomplished. "Thank you," Theo replied. "I know. I am."

Perceiving the exchange had run its course, Gachet nodded a few times and withdrew his hand. "You'll want to see him, of course. Take all the time you need." Stealing one last, lingering look at the figure on the bed, Gachet offered Theo an unconvincing smile before descending to the restaurant below.

Alone before the open door, Theo was possessed of a strange self-consciousness. He was cognisant of his body as an object in space and the sound of his breathing intruding upon the silence. Entering the room felt vaguely transgressive, like straying into the temple of a foreign faith. It was a place prepared for a rite that felt both oddly familiar and entirely incomprehensible. Exhaling deeply, he stepped inside.

The chamber was small and oppressive. Vincent lay unmoving on the bed. Ostensibly sleeping, he took no notice of his brother's entrance. Theo quietly approached the bedside. Vincent's face was white – very white. His hair was matted against his forehead with sweat, and his mouth was tight and scowled. Thin and delicate, his fingers clutched the bedclothes at unnatural angles. If he wasn't in pain now, it was obvious he had been recently.

The pathetic fragility of his brother's outstretched body, the uncanny contrast between this comatose figure and the man in the hospital, the vibrant, tender, infuriating man who was achingly sincere and so often wrong, the flooding awareness that he will never (never!) again be sincere or tender or wrong, the agonising knowledge that this harmless man had been wracked with more pain than he could possibly deserve (where, O God, is the justice in death that both the wicked and the righteous taste?), the uncomprehending pity expanding from his brother's broken form to include himself and Gachet and the men in the café and the women in the storefronts and everyone he ever met and didn't meet and children yet unborn, all of whom are destined to come to the same hopeless, miserable, unmerited end – it was all too much (too much to bear, too much to avoid), and Theo, holding his hand over his trembling mouth, began to cry.

Roused by the sound, Vincent slowly opened his eyes, confusion gradually giving way to recognition. "Forgive me," he sighed, making small movements with his fingers in the direction of his brother.

The shame of being comforted by his dying brother broke him open, and Theo began sobbing in earnest. He had failed him, was failing him.

"Forgive me," Vincent gently insisted, tears forming in the corners of his eyes. "The pain, the pain." He flinched. "It twists. It blinds. I can't go on. I would so like to go."

Through the pall of his sorrow, Theo began to grasp the situation. Smoothly and silently, his sadness began to slide back into a hidden chamber of his heart, like water down the drain of an unplugged basin. His weeping ceased and his breathing slowed as he stared at his brother.

"Forgive me," Vincent muttered. "Let me go. I can't go on. I would so like to go." His face was a wretched amalgam of distress and self-loathing. "I would so like to go."

Theo strained to parse the welter of emotions thrumming through him. He felt paralysed by a confluence of impulse: to weep, to scream, to flee, to beg, to break. Should he comfort the mewling patient in his arms or strangle the selfish bastard where he lies? He was furious not only at his brother's recklessness, but at his utter vulnerability, which cheated him out of an anger to which he felt justified. He did not know what to do. Inwardly reeling, he wished the heat would abate. He wished that doctor would do something, anything. And most of all, he wished none of this had ever happened.

Theo cast his eyes about the room, seeking some sign on how to proceed. As Vincent continued his incoherent murmuring, Theo noticed a small, red dot on the bedsheet, rising and falling with his brother's shallow breathing. Its colour and shape reminded him of a military decoration, like those awarded for valour in combat. With a kind of innocent fascination, he watched as the stain spread through the fibres of the cloth.

He reached out his hand and carefully peeled the bedclothes away. They clung to his brother's body with a revolting stickiness. Vincent's shirt – which had been cut down the front – hung on either side of his torso, revealing a taped bandage soaked with blood.

Vincent looked up into his brother's troubled face and followed his gaze back down to his chest. He seemed puzzled by the wound, as if he were seeing it for the first time. Lightly touching the dressing with his fingertips, he gradually seemed to recall the injury's origin. When he looked back at Theo, his eyes were shining serenely. The words were barely audible. "This is what I wanted."

Theo felt his heart sink. The deliberate certainty of his brother's words snuffed out the last, flickering glimmer of hope that – against his conscious will – he had long concealed in his breast. The sensation was oddly comfortable, like nestling into a dark, hollow burrow. He had finally been released from his responsibility – the bondage of his love – but he felt neither relief nor regret. He merely sensed he had enough life left to dig a grave – he had not the strength for two – and, having secreted his brother's remains in the all-consuming earth, expire upon its clovered cover.

Vincent soon fell into a coma from which he would not awake. The doctor was fetched, and the patient was made comfortable. However, it took hours for the stubborn animal to die. The body's dumb tenacity – its mute and irrepressible commitment to survival – held out well into the night. At times, he lay so still Theo could not be sure he hadn't slipped away without noticing. At others, his starving lungs sucked air into a gaping mouth with such violent desperation the windowpane rattled in resonance. Despite our resolution, death – Theo reflected – takes no man willingly.

As the darkness crept into the room, Theo unburdened himself. Over and over, he told Vincent that he loved him, that it would be alright, that he would carry on. With feeble perseveration, he confessed his trespasses – the smothered rage, the hesitant omissions – and begged his brother for forgiveness. He hoped the words would ease his passing, but if they did he could not tell. Vincent's ears were stuffed with a silence Theo's voice could not penetrate. Or was it his words – as words – were things too small and simple to convey the contents of his heart? What is "love" but a syllable? What part of forgiveness can be spoken? And who after all was he trying to reassure?

It was after midnight when Vincent finally succumbed in the presence of Theo and the doctor. After passing through all the body's hideous attempts to prolong its meagre existence, he expelled his last breath with a quiet groan. The body was cold in minutes. Already its resemblance to the living man was fading. He was gone. One minute, Theo had a brother. The next, he didn't.

He crossed over to the room's small window and opened it. As he attempted to make sense of how a person could travel such a vast and irrevocable distance so quickly, he looked up at the stars glinting over the village. He recalled Vincent's painting of the sky in Provence, and he tried to make his eyes see the night's swirling profusion –

but to no avail. If it existed, he could not see it. Searching the heavens, there were only the stars as he had ever known them: fixed, faint, and unfathomable.

ADELINE

Dear Diary,

Today is Monday. It will be my berthday in forteen days. Then Ceecee wont be older than me.

I ate bred and strawbery jam. I dint wash my plate becus I dint have to! Mommy told me to tell the man and I telled him. Then I plaid outside.

I walkt by the river. I saw a dog and too cats! One was blak and one was wite (with blak paws). It was hot but I dint swim.

Ceecee has a baby doll but she wont shair so I hate her. But if she shaird with me I wood be her frend. I wood be carefull.

At home there were peeple standing inside and they all lookt at me. Mommy told me I cood have a cookee if I went to my room. So I went to my room!

Pink is prittier than red but wite is prittier than pink.

Good nite. I will rite tommorow.

GACHET

12 May

While walking an unaccustomed trail this afternoon, I came upon a small rise that overlooked the valley below. I could at once survey the hopeful patchwork of the ripening fields, the pleasant disarray of the country village, and – wending its way through both – the gentle bend of the undulating river. An uncanny quiet stole over me, and I could feel a quickening in my blood. Standing there, I was filled with the mute but unmistakable certainty the scene was to serve as the subject of my next painting. Reeling with possibility, I returned home with a renewed sense of purpose. What sweet misfortune lay in store for me?

The post brought a letter from a contact I had met some time ago in Paris. He wrote to express his wish that I might become acquainted with his brother, who would soon be settling in Auvers. I have heard C. speak of this man on occasion. Apparently, he is also a painter of some ability, but who has as yet been unable to make a name for himself. I only pray he is not as discourteous as some of our more recent transplants, whose conceit so poorly compensates their lack of success.

14 May

Three patients, all neurasthenic. The train seems to deliver more from the city every day. At this rate, it is only a matter of time before our village is overrun with exhausted bourgeoisie. They are Paris's chief export. A lamentable necessity, I suppose, as there are fewer places better suited to soothe the discordant nerves of the urban-afflicted than our humble village. Prescribed fresh air and bed rest.

The heightened incidence of such disorders is obviously alarming, and it is difficult to ignore their unmistakable concentration in city centres. Though certain technologies have clearly enhanced our capacities for productivity, it grows increasingly undeniable these advances come at a cost. The telegraph may have conquered space. The electric light may have dispelled the dark. But are not space and dark essential to a human organism that evolved within their confines? It would seem as though humanity's drive to create perpetually outstrips its ability to adapt. And any creature ill-suited to its environment is bound to suffer. Perhaps this is inescapable. Even Prometheus bought fire with his liver.

20 May

I spent the morning with M., who is still feeling poorly. She has always been a girl of delicate constitution, but her fragility of late is more pronounced than usual. Sent for bone broth to stimulate the blood, but she ate very little. Concerning.

I received a caller in the afternoon. To my surprise, it was the artist (V.) whose acquaintance I had been begged to make. Apparently, he knew nothing of Auvers except my name and address and had come straight from the station upon arriving, his valise still in tow. For some reason, he was possessed of the curious conviction I was at his disposal to facilitate his change of residence. Were his association not recommended to me by those whose taste I respect, I might have rankled at such a presumption. Then again, perhaps this is not so unusual. If nothing else, my experience has taught me eccentricity so often attends genius that I fear I may now doubt the existence of the latter if unaccompanied by the former.

As I had already concluded my business for the day, I offered to escort him into town for lunch. As we smoked after our meal, he spoke on his hopes for the future, which mainly consisted of an earnest desire to live simply in the pursuit of his art. Charming, if a bit naïve. He made no mention of his psychiatric history, which omission resulted in some otherwise mystifying gaps in his narrative. A portion of his left ear was missing. Whether he sat in profile to hear my words or hide his disfigurement is unclear. I referred him to a nearby inn and agreed to view his work once he was sufficiently settled.

Walking back, I considered my first impressions of the man. It was neither his passion nor his impetuousness – both of which were clearly evident and may, after all, spring from the same source – but his defencelessness that was most striking. I could sense none of the caution that usually attends a social introduction. He spoke to me as if we were confidants who had long enjoyed a close intimacy. His trust in me was flattering, seductive. Had I so desired his heart's true confession, I doubt he would have objected. He may have been gratified someone wanted to hear it.

M. was sleeping when I returned. I did not wake her.

21 May

V. returned after breakfast. I was in my study, contemplating how to achieve a particular shade of orange with the pigments I had on hand, when I heard the knock on my door. He was exuberant, giddy, and all but insisted I come by his room to see his paintings. As he had only just arrived and had brought with him little by way of personal effects, I assumed he misspoke. Sketches, perhaps – but surely not paintings. I assured him I would call in the afternoon.

When I arrived at his quarters, I was dismayed to find he had not taken my recommendation, choosing instead to lodge in shabbier accommodations. Indeed, the room was the archetypal artist's garret: atmospheric, if not a bit clichéd. When I arrived, he was fussing over a small canvas – a chestnut tree bursting with blooms – which he was pleased to present to me. When I expressed my amazement that he had already completed a painting, he informed me it was – in fact – his second, having finished a still life of one of the tree's fallen branches the night before. He set them both on his easel.

It is difficult to relate my internal state upon seeing his work for the first time. I can recall a jolt of excitement, a quickening of the heart, a shiver of fear. The paintings tempted me, challenged me. The technique was simple, but not simplistic. The composition, balanced and unaffected. Looking raised questions further looking resolved. Nearly every brushstroke lay visible on the canvas. The longer I gazed, the more clearly I could reconstruct the exact sequence of steps by which the images were brought into being. The paintings simultaneously depicted created objects – a tree, a branch – and the process by which they were created. They showed a world that both had once been and was in the midst of becoming. And it was this contrast – like the tension between focus and field – that cultivated in me something akin to fascination.

I confess I remember little of our subsequent conversation. I believe we spoke on the weather and other local concerns. While attempting to satisfy his appetite for information, I contended with my own burgeoning obsession. Who was this young man? The paintings I had viewed were afterthoughts, improvisations. They were thrown together as an afternoon's pastime – and yet they were more technically accomplished than anything now hanging in Montmartre. Genius is as rare as it is deceptive: a mirage that has led countless astray. And yet V. had literally arrived on my doorstep. Were my eyes beguiled by a fateful desire or were they seeing the unlikely truth?

As I looked into his ruddy face, I could sense my resolution growing. Yes, I could see clearly. Yes, I would trust my judgement. Yes, I had reason to believe. Incredibly – miraculously – I stood before an oasis in the desert. And why not? Such places must after all exist. They make passage through life's wastes possible.

29 May

Since apprising myself of his ability, I have become determined to spend as much time with V. as possible. And as he has no other known associates in Auvers, he has for his part – I think – been grateful for my company. In less than a fortnight, he has become a regular fixture in my home, arriving in the afternoon and – on more than one occasion – staying well into the evening.

As the weather has been so clement, we have developed a custom of sitting in the garden, smoking and discussing any manner of things. Like an overripe fruit, his mind is bursting with ideas, the pulpy pith of which he naturally prefers to the tasteless rind of convention. In conversation, he demonstrates a marked distaste for social pleasantries and a complete abhorrence for all form of pretence – both of which remind me of a younger version of myself. The artlessness of his character – in conjunction, perhaps, with the reputation of my profession – have conspired to create the kind of ardent friendship that typically requires years to forge.

Nearly every day he presents me with another of his new works, and in turn I have begun to introduce him to my own poor productions, which he has received warmly. Though initially wary of his presence, M. has begun joining us for these informal exhibitions. It would seem as though the looked-for close of an overlong spring has improved her condition. As for V., he continues to paint as though it were not the season, but time itself that was approaching its conclusion. Does he sleep? But with Armageddon on the morrow, what man could?

2 June

After learning of my phrenological studies, V. consented to a cranial examination. As might be expected, he exhibited protuberances in many regions associated with visual perception (12, 13, 16, &c.), which finding – I believe – helped to confirm him in the veracity of the discipline. Most intriguing was the presence of nodules in the areas devoted to both destructiveness and veneration (i.e., 5 and 31). While I have often encountered ridges in the former region – in the impressions made of the skulls, for example, of executed criminals – they have always been accompanied by depressions in the latter. This is the first time I have observed such a puzzling combination.

How to reconcile these opposing drives? Would the characterological impulse be to destroy what one worships or to worship what one destroys? Both seem paradoxical. I suppose the answer rests on whether the intention is to expiate guilt or eliminate inadequacy. While I can sense in V. the memory of no great moral transgression, I can neither find any evidence of a neurotic preoccupation with self. If anything, he seems objective in his own self-assessment: cognisant of his talent, without recourse to either overweening grandiosity or false humility.

I have found that men of his quality are often possessed of a singular sensitivity. The same exquisite capacity for feeling both uplifts and casts down. Much as the charming allure of the everyday – the play of light and shadow under an oak tree, the candid line of a barmaid's profile – goes unnoticed by the mass of humanity, so too do the painful absurdities that underscore our existence go unfelt by the same. This may be the justice that tempers the otherwise inequitable distribution of ability. And yet what man would refuse to pay such a cost? What price is too high for such a priceless gift? Perhaps – as Dante understood – the grace to ascend to the heavens is only awarded to those first willing to descend into hell. The capacity to suffer may well be the badge of the elect.

9 June

Today V. began to paint on the premises. As it has become his habit to spend so much of his time here, it felt only natural to extend him such an invitation. It has – so far – proven to be a happy arrangement. He is provided a tranquil environment in which to work undisturbed, and I am allowed an opportunity to observe his process *in situ*.

It was his pleasure to make a portion of my garden the subject of his first work. Sitting beneath an alder at some remove, I was able to witness its creation over the course of two pipes. His movements were confident, definitive. He paints with a fearsome focus, as if he were searching out a quiet voice in a crowded room. Indeed, if the painting weren't clearly depicting the sight before me, I would attest he listened more than looked, receiving his instruction from the voice of an unseen master.

When he finished, we drank wine while the oils dried in the afternoon sun. A faint breeze rustled the overarching foliage, lending the scene a winsome sweetness. The soft haze of intoxication settled gently on my senses, and the world was reborn – redeemed – in the fading light of day. We spoke of love and art, dreams and visions: of the beauty that instills in man the courage to face the darkness. If death still lived, he stalked not here, in my little garden, another Eden, bounded with a hedge. And as the stars appeared, they winked in approval of a truth once forgotten, now reclaimed: the gates of heaven float but a finger's breadth above the ground.

12 June

As summer continues to lengthen its days, my routine has assumed a languid rhythm befitting the season. In the morning, I attend to my patients. In the evening, I converse with V. And I devote any spare moments to M. She has made a wondrous recovery. It gladdens my heart to see her face now flush with the healthy glow of youth. When we chat in the garden about her girlish fancies and innocent discoveries, I cannot help but feel as though we are living in the halcyon days. So replete are the hours with a muted joy that – if I do not wrest myself, on occasion, from their tender spell – they will have slipped away, unremembered.

I stole away for an hour to work on my landscape this evening. At dusk, the sky fluoresced with an uncommon radiance, bathing the countryside in a limpid gold. So beautiful it was the wind stood still and the birds ceased their chatter. It was as if nature itself was rapt in the contemplation of her own loveliness. Contending with my own mounting awe, I attempted to capture the moment while it lived. If I succeeded in portraying even a fraction of its brilliance, then the piece may yet be worth looking at.

20 June

When he arrived this afternoon, V. proposed I sit for a portrait. Though I initially demurred, he would not be dissuaded, insisting he be allowed to requite my hospitality this past month. What could I do? The prospect of being painted by V. filled me with a kind of elated trepidation. What concealed truth would his vision reveal? Would I recognise its depiction in myself? We decorated a small table and moved it into the garden, where I attempted to strike a natural pose.

The ordeal was blessedly brief. Attending the spectacle in a white sundress, M. monitored the painting's progress with a good deal of enthusiasm, occasionally releasing a squeal of delight that did little to allay my apprehension. Fortunately, these outbursts did not appear to distract V., who continued to work with an unflinching focus.

The experience was unsettling. In his gaze, I could sense no acknowledgment of my person, which – unreflected – seemed to disappear. Perhaps there was no self to see: only the outward forms of line and shape and hue. My individuality was only an illusion created by some cunning technique, like depth on a canvas. Any anxiety I harboured over viewing the completed work was overshadowed by the relief I felt when he had finished painting.

M. considers the portrait an unmitigated success, and she has already secured a steadfast commitment from V. that she might be his next subject. It is clear the painting is both visually interesting and technically accomplished – though

I admit I may be unable to judge its merits dispassionately. However, there is a sadness on the canvas I cannot identify in myself. They say husband and wife come to resemble each other over the long course of their marriage. Could the years of accompanying the struggles of others have transformed the features of my face? Or am I simply responding to the unmistakable fact – depicted with neither cruelty nor malice – that I am no longer young?

As today marked the summer solstice, we lingered in the garden and discussed the meaning of the time. Life's only constant is change, and the wheel – now perched upon a glorious zenith – must begin its implacable descent. The light will recede to return to recede. But this is no cause for concern: all things are renewed in its cycle. For now, however, the wheat is still growing, and there is wine yet to drink. Here, there is no winter, and time enough remains for our mortal designs. As I spoke, V. listened intently in the twilight.

24 June

In reviewing my recent entries, it is evident V. has exerted a powerful influence over my thoughts of late. I will not deny our exchanges constitute the better part of my days. I imagine the feeling is akin to the exhilaration a man who has spent his life in the desert might feel upon first seeing the ocean: the existence of a long-unmet need is revealed in its sudden satisfaction.

That said, my compulsion to document our interactions is not entirely a private impulse. I find myself increasingly possessed of the certainty that V. will one day be recognised as a Great Man. And by some mysterious providence, I have been afforded an unobstructed vantage from which to observe the goings-on of his life. As such, I feel duty-bound to create this record of our relationship for posterity, over and above any personal considerations. Though it could be this inkling is little more than the new expression of an old vanity.

Today, it was our pleasure to walk beside the Oise. A breeze played upon the surface of the languid water, gently agitating the reflection of the clouds above. I don't know whether it was the tasteful pageantry of that pastoral scene or the comforting presence of a trustworthy friend that set V. at his ease, but he began – unprompted – to relate the particulars concerning his tenure at the various mental institutions at which he had been a guest. I listened with a more than professional interest.

Given the cures he underwent, I would assume he had been diagnosed by a well-meaning – but potentially incompetent – physician with a *folie circulaire*: a judgement for which I have personally found little corroborating evidence. Apparently, some of V.'s attending doctors even considered his prolificacy to be a sign of lunacy! I commiserated. It is everywhere the fate of genius to be misapprehended by lesser natures. At least, I reminded him, he had not been subjected to some of the brutal treatments that are still practised in La Salpêtrière to our considerable discredit. I was encouraged to learn he possessed more than a little interest in my promising research in the field of clinical homeopathy, which I related in some detail.

When it came time for us to part, V. complained of a mild headache. As a sign of goodwill, I provided him a remedy of my own creation: a potentised tincture of digitalis, staphysagria, and opium.

27 June

After a few days of temperamental weather, during which time I contented myself with some of the more solitary pursuits of my study, the moody heavens – having exhausted their bluster – finally opened. The entire countryside was suffused with a charming freshness, as though the rain had washed away the dross of ages past to reveal a second youth – lovely and bright – now clamouring for the acknowledgment that is beauty's rightful due from the human soul.

When V. returned, we agreed it would be an ideal moment to compose M.'s portrait in the garden. Planted among the roses in her white dress, she looked like a blossom herself, pale and mild. As she posed, I couldn't help but laugh at her innocent attempts to appear pleasingly uncontrived. It wasn't long, however, before this clumsy artifice started to dissolve into impatience, and she began to fidget with the coquettishness unique to understimulated girls. If his model's fussing bothered him, V. gave no sign of his vexation. Indeed, he carried on with his customary vigor and all but collapsed once the painting was complete. His shirt was wet with the sweat of his strain. Rushing over to view the finished result – the oils still glistening in the sun – M. offered her most enthusiastic approval before skipping away to parts unknown. V. lit a pipe and reclined against the trunk of my chestnut.

As we conversed in the shade, the discourse gradually descended from the rarefied realms where we are inclined to soar in favor of more worldly concerns. The portrait of M. would be a gift for my daughter, but did I not know anyone who might be interested in buying one of his recent works? When I told him – despite its reputation – there were few true patrons of the arts in Auvers, he looked perplexed and proceeded to proposition me directly. I replied that I was reluctant to adulterate the purity of our friendship – which was far more precious than a few francs – with a financial transaction. I went on to assure him I was much better suited for a role as fellow artist and ardent supporter than that of formal patron, which – in any case – I hadn't the means to fulfil. And I reminded him it was only a matter of time before he received the recognition he deserved, encouraging him to consider his stay in Auvers as a kind of residency in preparation for his future fame. After I had finished, he smoked a while in silence.

When he spoke again, it was on a completely different subject. Though he attempted to cover his reaction with a mask of indifference, V. remained abstracted and withdrawn for the rest of the conversation until – inventing some convenient pretext – he excused himself for the evening. In the privacy of these pages, I must confess my disappointment. All the gold in existence could not purchase an ounce of V.'s talent. Is not the exercise of that skill sufficient recompense? Surely such a virtue must be its own considerable reward.

For all their brilliance, the creations of other eras were clouded by a kind of cravenness: the willingness to bend the knee, kiss the ring. Only the productions of the present day have succeeded in separating themselves from this distasteful servility. For the first time in history, we are in possession of an art for its own sake: authentic and pure. Let lesser men be satisfied with more.

30 June

Returning with M. from our morning constitutional, we found V. awaiting us at the front gate. It was earlier than his wonted time to call, and he was dressed more formally than usual. Though he greeted us warmly, there was a weariness in his expression, as if his eyes had not lately seen sleep. Startled by the unlooked-for guest, M. seemed flustered and quickly took her leave, while the two of us for a change of pace settled ourselves in the parlour.

I could see V. was ill at ease. He pawed at the remnants of his ear, and more than once he turned in his chair as though he half-expected to find someone watching him from the corner of the room. Believing he may still feel embarrassed after our recent exchange, I tried to assure him his request hadn't diminished my affection in the slightest. However, he only looked confused, apparently having already forgotten the incident to which I was referring.

As his present condition would have betrayed any claims to the contrary, V. confessed he had not been sleeping of late. He continues to produce new work at an astonishing rate, occasionally filling more than one canvas in the span of a day. When pressed as to the secret driver of his prolixity, he responded cryptically: "The day wears long." He gave the impression of a man who is chronically dissatisfied with his own efforts – a disposition all true artists seem to share.

He began to question me about my research. Though I am generally reluctant to discuss my work, I could sense a note of desperation in V.'s repeated entreaties I could only with deliberate unkindness ignore. After reviewing the lamentable deficiencies in my profession's response to melancholic illness – the treatment of which is sadism masquerading as medicine – I discussed the various elements that actually constitute an effective cure: hard work, purposeful action, and meaningful relations.

To my surprise, V. grew increasingly agitated as I spoke. Unable to restrain himself any longer, he interrupted my discourse on the benefits of sunshine, insisting – in so many words – such treatments were neither adequate for prevention nor effective as remedy. The forcefulness of his interjection was such that I was temporarily left at a want for words. Perhaps realising from my stunned silence he had acted with more vehemence than necessary, he proceeded to slink back in his chair and withdraw into himself.

Despite my efforts to engage him in conversation, V. remained inaccessible. Like calling to someone on the deck of a departing ship, my words were swallowed by the intervening air. While I considered how best to salvage the situation, he suddenly rose from his seat and – without a word of explanation – very nearly ran out of the room.

I did not pursue him. Indeed, I remained in the parlour for some time, sitting with my misgivings. When I had my fill of these unfriendly thoughts, I got up from my chair and crossed over to the picture window. Behind the proscenium of ivy, I could see M. and V. in the garden, like characters in a play. Wearing an empty expression, M. was walking toward the conservatory, down right. While V., head down and back hunched, slowly made his way upstage toward a painted backdrop of distant hills.

3 July

Good light today. I was able to make some progress on the landscape in the afternoon. I believe it will be one of my better offerings once I resolve the matter of the central tree. For some reason, it appears too stubborn, too willful. I can't seem to make it accord with the rest of the piece, which is otherwise possessed of an agreeable harmony.

If the problem lies in me, then the solution does, as well. I am confident this is only a temporary setback.

7 July

As it had been a week since V.'s unceremonious departure, and having not received any communication from him to allay my concern, I made up my mind to call on him directly. I did so after breakfast. He welcomed me bashfully and cleared a rumpled mass of clothes from a chair for me to sit. The little room was dim and disordered, and empty bottles of absinthe lay strewn about the floor. Since he did not initially attend to me, instead moving about the apartment in a half-hearted attempt at tidying up, it took me a few minutes to realise he was drunk.

When I finally prevailed on him to settle down, he perched on the edge of the bed and regarded me mournfully. His eyes were damp and clouded, like a silty stream. Though we sat so close to each other our knees fairly touched, I had the distinct impression he was inwardly elsewhere, living through the kind of experience that is recalled more clearly the more one tries to forget.

He spoke through the haze of a maudlin nostalgia, reminiscing about our friendship as if it were a thing long past. Though I maintained he did nothing – could do nothing – to sap the strength of our bond, his ears were deaf to my repeated entreaties. Indeed, they only fixed him more firmly in his conviction to the contrary. Despite my mounting discomfort, he repeatedly insisted that I was a good man with a good heart, that the world was better for my being in it, and many other commendations to similar effect. As a mound is heaped high with the contents of a corresponding pit, he seemed to sink lower and lower as his praise piled up. Until finally – having reached the nadir of his self-abasement – he abandoned his unhappy task and succumbed to the full force of his feelings.

He wept brutally, viciously – his chest heaving like the pitiless swells that beat upon the storm-addled coast. Through gasping breaths, he recited his failings, real and imagined. He was unworthy, unlovable. He was a failure, a fraud. A broken human being subsisting on the pity of others. A miserable fool only good for terrifying women. A useless idiot whose best was not good enough. An incurable lunatic incapable of the simplest tasks. A wicked deceiver, and a degenerate besides. A drunk. He insisted he did not deserve to exist. With each new invective, his voice rose in volume and pitch until – approaching the limits of his register – his speech collapsed into breathless incoherence.

I sat by helplessly. Like weathering a cloudburst in some unexpected place, there is little to be done in such moments but wait. Searching for shelter, I cast my eyes about the room and noticed a small painting propped against the wainscoting. A village lay beneath a swirling, spangled sky. The little outpost looked exposed and defenceless under the massive heavens, which seemed prepared to draw the town – brick and stone and steeple – into its devouring maelstrom. A cypress tree had already begun its rapturous ascent. What would remain of the nameless settlement? And who would remember it once existed in futile defiance of that all-consuming nature?

Looking back at V., I was filled with melancholy. This mewling man, this dismal room, this torrid scene, charged with urgent passion begging for release: what did it amount to? We move through time like a knife across the water, our trackless path effaced no sooner than it's made. Yet who would trade this little life for the boundless deep? And so we cling to sodden straws like shipwrecked sailors and pray they'll raft us but a minute more. We are not built to float. And our eyes look ever upward as we sink.

8 July

V. came to apologise – hat in hand – this afternoon. Though he had apparently travelled to the villa for this express purpose, he refused my invitation to come inside, casting a wary glance at the space beyond the threshold. Standing awkwardly in the afternoon sun, he delivered a halting plea to be delivered from the sin of his embarrassment.

After assuring the mumbling penitent he had committed no offence worth mentioning, I exploited the opportunity afforded by his presumed sobriety. Melancholia – like a pale torch – can both enlighten and encinder. The use to which it is applied depends on the discipline of the patient and his capacity to abide in pain. Perhaps it is his doom to suffer, but the same God who has meted out his grief has apportioned him a talent in equal measure. By exercising that great gift, he can transform his plight into light, ransom himself from an unjust fate ...

I had not the heart to continue. Each successive sentence only served to bewilder him further, his face gradually hardening into a mask of terrified incomprehension. He looked like a traveller lost in a foreign land whose further progress depended on directions he could not understand. We stared at each other uncomfortably until he turned to go, as though suddenly ashamed of his own presence. Watching V. stumble down the road, I searched my heart for the words that would call him back – but could find none that would suffice. I am at a loss even now, several hours later.

We would not feed a starving man a picture of food. And yet we expect our words to sustain each other. What folly! There is no gift except the thing itself. So we trade in words to hide our ignorance. For who among us knows the subtle diet of the soul?

12 July

Though I do not know the cause, I cannot deny M. has lately fallen into distraction. Her vibrant cheer – only recently restored – has once more been covered by a contemplative pall. Our daily walks are stamped with silence, and my fumbling attempts to draw her out fall soundly on deaf ears. She seems sad and weary, like one much older who, having seen too many winters, must suffer through another still.

I am convinced no man is lonelier than the father of a distant daughter. She walks beside him on paths he cannot follow.

15 July

Last night, I dreamt one of my patients – I did not recognise his face – was convinced the sky was made of glass. He spoke in such a way as to presume my agreement, as if we were discussing a widely accepted fact. Lamentably, those around him did not share his perception, and he was feeling increasingly frustrated and isolated in their disbelief. He confessed he was even starting to question his own sanity. Desperate and distraught, he sought my advice on how he might persuade his friends and relations to accept the obvious truth.

I proceeded cautiously, dancing around the delusion. Sensing my hesitation, the man grew confused, then suspicious, then impatient – eventually demanding I disclose my stance on the matter. When I gently revealed my position, the man became irate and ran out of the office. Following him into the garden, I watched as he picked up a stone and hurled it into the heavens. With a thunderous crack, the sky shattered like a chandelier. As the gleaming shards rained down around us, he turned to me – vindicated – before falling to his knees in dawning realisation of what he had just done.

I woke up at this point, breathing heavily in the dark. The moonlight silvering the sheets served as a speechless sign the sky still stood. Like sand through a glass, the memory of the dream began to fade, only to be replaced with a growing sense I was not alone. Just as one is occasionally possessed of the uncanny sensation of being watched in some public place, only to look up in time to see a stranger quickly avert his eyes, I could feel an unfamiliar presence lurking somewhere in the house. Straining my ears, I could make out the muffled shuffling of furtive movement as I quietly rose to seek its source.

Following the sound into my study, I entered upon a frightful scene. The large picture window facing the garden had been smashed, and its fragments littered the floor. Papers fluttered about the room like long-imprisoned birds released from their cages. Heaps of books, upended from their orderly stacks, lay sprawled like the ruins of Babel upon the ground. In the midst of this profusion, swaying unsteadily, stood V., the portrait of M. under his arm. Bathed in the spectral light of the moon, he looked eerily insubstantial, as though he would vanish completely if he stepped into the shadows.

I called out his name as he began to stumble toward the window. Alerted to my presence, he spun around with the panicked eyes of a schoolboy discovered in his mischief. When he realised he could not hide the painting behind his back, he let it fall to the floor in a gesture of contemptuous resignation. As we stared at each other in the gloom, he took a staggering step toward me, his mouth twisted into a scornful sneer. Then, like a swollen stream surmounting its shores, he unleashed a torrent of abuse that must have long yearned for an outlet.

He called me a charlatan, a quack whose worthless cures preyed upon the hopeful, and he assured me I was at least as mad as he. My painting was a sham, amateurish at best, and my attempts to associate with actual artists did nothing to mask my mediocrity. Too much of a coward to live my own life, I fed on the second-hand passions of others, like some mental parasite. I could turn the most mundane observation into a self-important lecture. I was pretentious and pedantic, oblivious to those around me, a bankrupt intellectual and a dilettante besides. I would never create anything of real value. Finally, he accused me of exploiting his talent for my own personal gain.

Whether he was satisfied with his salvo or had run out of ammunition, I do not know. However, he paused there, eyes feral and bright, and awaited my retort. When he saw I had none to offer, he gave a small, derisive laugh and turned to go. Lurching wildly, he collided with my desk, knocking a sheaf of papers to the floor. He then picked up an ashtray and threw it in my general direction, before falling through the broken window. Disappearing from sight, he seemed swallowed by the night itself.

I stood there unmoving, not knowing what to think or how to feel. My disparate emotions struggled with their own contradictions for expression. Pique and pity each demanded satisfaction. Bathos and betrayal both imposed upon my heart. An abundance of impulse compelled my stillness. Until finally, as though moving of its own accord, my body began to pick up the papers scattered across the floor. The gesture did little to constrain the chaos that reigned upon that room. But what could I do? How else does one restore a fallen keep? It is a bitter truth that even man's most noble works are composed of small and senseless acts. And it is merely the scope of our focus that determines the salvation of our souls.

22 July

It took a week for V. to return. I immediately recognised his knock, the timid rapping of an uncertain supplicant, and bade M. retreat to her bedroom. An afterimage of our confrontation flashed before my mind's eye, and I could sense my pulse begin to quicken. Though I was reluctant to engage with him, I would not be a prisoner of fear in my own home. Once more I would be the bigger man. Pride is expensive: to afford it we must abstain from lesser sins.

I met him on the threshold. Any tension I had been holding in expectation of this encounter vanished on sight. His change in appearance was so complete I could hardly recognise him as the same man who had torn like a tempest through my study just a few days ago. He did not ask to be invited in, and I did not offer. Instead he proceeded, in calm and measured tones, to apologise for his previous behavior.

He admitted he needed help and declared he would no longer allow his arrogance to prevent him from asking his brother for assistance. He recognised his problematic relationship with alcohol and – five days sober – assured me he was committed to his continued abstinence. He informed me his intention was to return to the asylum in Saint-Rémy, where he could prioritise his recovery without adding to the burdens of others. And though he lacked the funds to do so at the present time, he promised to compensate me for the destruction of my property once he managed to sell one of his paintings.

It was a stunning reversal. He was sincere without sentiment, accountable without cringing. The entire confession was perhaps the most perfect apology I had ever received. And as I closed the door on this strange episode, I felt like a captive released from long-accustomed shackles: grateful, relieved, and unsure as to why he fears his own delivery.

29 July

There are moments in a man's life that are etched into his heart. Impressed with the force of an uncommon emotion, they alter the course of his days thereafter. The birth of a daughter, the death of a wife. These events mark time in the life of an individual as profoundly as the advent of Our Saviour divided humanity's history in twain. This was one of those moments.

I was asleep when the knocking roused me. Against the low rumbling of a summer squall, the sharp notes echoed dissonantly through the darkened house. Expecting a gendarmes to be the author of such an importunate sound, I was startled to find the master of the Auberge Ravoux, drenched and bedraggled, standing in the doorway. He bade me follow him, quickly. I grabbed my Gladstone, threw a coat over my house clothes, and slipped into the night.

On the hurried path into town, shouting through the curtain of rain, he told me V. had returned to the inn that evening later than usual, soiled with mud and blood. When queried, V. apparently confessed he had shot himself with suicidal intent. Leaving his wife to attend on him, the innkeeper came to fetch me straightaway. Almost as an afterthought, he informed me V. might already be dead. As we entered the village, I offered a wordless prayer to God and braced myself for what I would encounter in that miserable garret.

I found V. slouched against his headboard. A pang of uncomprehending terror shot through me at the sight of him: the same panicked revulsion all good men must feel when confronted with the wanton destruction of something beautiful. Upon my arrival, he exhaled slowly as if accommodating to the inevitability of my presence. His shirt was soaked through with blood, and his pale face shimmered with perspiration. Though he remained possessed of thought, his evident pain tolerance indicated he was likely in the grip of a psychotic episode – a hypothesis that was subsequently confirmed by the tenor of his speech.

He was initially reluctant for me to examine him, but his weakened state could afford only feeble resistance. Cutting away his shirt, I immediately identified the entry wound: a red crater dusted black beneath his heart. I could find no corresponding puncture elsewhere on his body. Palpating his abdomen, I deduced the round was likely lodged in his stomach, rendering the wound inoperable. With the tools at my disposal, attempting an extraction would only succeed in hastening his demise. If the bullet merely nicked the organ, there was a chance he could survive. As silent tears slid down my cheeks, I cleaned the wound as best I could, bade him take a dose of laudanum, and fell into the chair opposite.

The presence of death compels honesty more than the force of any legal oath. All secrets are buried with the body. As the room assumed the hushed solemnity of a sleepless night, he asked – in a small voice – if I was disappointed in him. It was pointless to lie: the dismay was conveyed in every line of my face. Looking as the life slowly seeped out of him, I might as well have been watching the collapse of an empire or the burning of some ancient library. I told him I was, and he gave me a sad smile. He said his life was his to do with as he pleased, and no man had the right to compel the continued existence of one that had become unbearable.

Anger flared inside me like a sudden sun. The selfishness, the spitefulness, the brazen wastefulness of suicide are hard enough to tolerate without their shameless endorsement. I felt like a starving man forced to watch a child step on bread. Did he not realise the crumbs he despised would sustain another? Men strive for years to attain a fraction of what he was freely given, and his future – so lately forfeit – yet contained more wonders than the works of ages past. To simply exist – to be even the meanest creature – is an incomprehensible blessing, a gift beyond price. How could he be so violent with life?

On the contrary, he replied, it was life that had been so violent with him. His decision was not an act of aggression, but one of surrender. The world had no place for him.

Whether this was despite his genius or because of it made little difference: the result remained the same. He was to live below men or beyond them – but not among them. That his fellows would consign him to such a lonely post was harsh enough. But to be disparaged for abandoning a hopeless station by those who would expend no effort in his rescue was the height of cruelty. The spectator would not have his fighter fall, but neither does he feel his blows.

No one, I conceded, can weigh the suffering of another, but it was an affront to God to seize for oneself His lawful privilege. Man has no right to destroy what he did not create. His life does not belong to him. It is only his to enjoy until the time appointed for its return. Our highest duty is to restore without complaint a spirit made more perfect through our struggles. Relief from a moment that would have soon passed – and was, in any case, in the service of that perfection – is terrible recompense for one's undying soul.

He admitted – if he had made a fool's bargain – it was because he was a fool, a wretched fool. And yet he died trusting in God's judgement and His mercy. The former, he explained, would not expect a fool to act wise, while the latter could not abandon him in his agony. Perpetual separation from a god without these attributes would hardly qualify as hell, as such a place would resemble nothing so much as the world in which we already lived. His god could not be the living source of truth if he punished those who earnestly pursued these goods along their untravelled paths.

Back and forth, we spoke in such a fashion through the night until – with the coming of the dawn – his responses grew too faint and dim to hear. Not once did he complain about his pain. Not once did he rue his fatal decision. He bore the conscious process of his passing with gallant restraint and a noble resignation. If the truest measure of a man is how he bears up in the face of death – death not as some abstract principle or universal fate, but as his own personal annihilation – then V. possessed a greatness of spirit rarely encountered among the common run. Such magnanimity can only be acquired in the place an ordinary man is too loath to look: the crucible of his own suffering.

The sun was already high by the time V.'s brother arrived from the city to comfort the dying man. Over the course of our brief interaction, he revealed himself to be both unprepared and unremarkable. But blood is blood: it owes the duty it pays to itself. Yielding him the only chair, I retreated to the café to organise my thoughts. However, the overloud conversations of the other patrons irked me. A man – a great man! – was dying upstairs. How could they persist in their insipid exchange? Yet that is the banality of death, which is an indifferent fact to all but the individuals in question.

When I returned to the room, V. had already slipped away – though his body yet persisted in its stubborn operation. I have seen the gasping husks of men too many times to feel the horror they naturally inspire. Deprived of the spirit, the body is a pulsating golem: a monstrous thing. However, this grotesqueness confirms my belief in the eternal life of man more than any sermon could. Man is the animating force, the flake of divine fire, and he returns on formless paths from whence he came. Why mourn that which never dies?

Yet I grieve the loss of this fool, this friend. For the world is darker without his ember in it, and I must journey on alone.

30 July

Today I destroyed the landscape I had been painting. I dug a pit in my garden and wordlessly watched it burn. I was hoping for some catharsis, some relief from the anguish that pressed upon my heart, but the pyre did nothing to dislodge my sorrow. The piece was soon reduced to smouldering ash. And among the cinders, no residue remained but a memory of warmth and light.

MARGUERITE

Dear Vincent,

Thank you for the lovely note. I wish to express my gratitude for having been given the opportunity to become acquainted with you these past weeks. You are truly a gifted painter, and I will treasure the portrait you made of me forever. Thank you for your kindness. You have a good heart, and I am honored to call you my friend.

I am not a particularly interesting woman. I have ordinary thoughts and ordinary desires. I know nothing about art. A man such as yourself would become bored with me. You deserve someone who could better accompany your unique talents.

Though I cannot give you what you seek, I am certain you shall make another woman very happy. Please know I wish you every blessing and hold you in the highest regard.

Sincerely,

Marguerite

dark

      wet

            underwater

                        waves and   light(?)

            the moon

                          getting bigger rising up

     (let me stay, let me stay)

                              rushing surging breaking

                       through

                 spinning and reeling

                         falling

                no

            gasping and flailing

                  drowning

                       no

        splitting and shaking

              bleeding

                   [opens eyes]

green on grey

         softly shifting

    (a watercolour)

             focus   returns

                   form

             retracts depth and

                         distance

(turf and trees)

            i remember

   on the ground

         rain

      water pooling   spilling into eye and ear

  light

wavers   sound

<pre>
                          warbles   the earth
                                 sighs   the smell
                                      of grass and grain
                          i remember
        hand to heart
               (flash of light)
          one two
             coat of blood
                               three four
                                breathing deep
                                              five six
                                         stab of pain
                                                   seven eight
              (roll of thunder)
                        it is comfortable
                                        to lie here
           sinking in the mud
                               soaked and tattered
                 cracked and leaking
                                                        alone
                                     under clash and cloud
                          finally
               i am safe
                                         i cannot sink
                                                further
                 what harm can befall me
                                     now?
          i am finished
                                         with anxious hope
                 and practiced dread
                                i will not fly
                     from fate   a moment more
</pre>

the boundary has been
                broken
                                  the night comes pouring in
half-drowned
        bleeding out
                        discarded chaff   in a forgotten field
                                      never have i felt
                                                      so alive
i see what my eyes can see
                a stalk of wheat   the whirling sky
                i hear what my ears can hear
                          my shallow breath   the whining wind
    sensations
            press upon me   close
                        and incomprehensible
                                          i am filled
                            with their forms   understanding
                                                      nothing
        (what is written in the rain?)
                        each drop
            empty
                                    and irreplaceable
                        each second
        a phoenix fire
        (how to grasp what has no handles?)
                                        to be
                                merely
                                        completely
        (   )
                always sated   ever hungry
                                              lightpacked eyes
                            soundstuffed ears

each pore   an unhinged
gate
the senses   ravenous and yielding
kindled nerves   in searing
circulation
feeling flares and fades to flare again
we are
combustion
(mosaics of light)
burning with beautiful finality
(the sun reborn)
in the fire's hollow heart
(where does it lie?)
the self asleep to self
(around the swirling waters, a drain)
the body being
breathing
pure perception
(the rose before we learnt its name)
the feeling of what is
no more
no less
(meaning, a labyrinth, untangled)
could this be   heaven?
[turns on back]
columns of light
r e a c h I n g u p
to hang the stars
(a drop to fall, a rope to climb)
here i lay
a blade of grass
a pebble

smooth-worn by time

and indifference

drinking in the grace

of non-being

* * *

if i had known

dying would feel   like this

i would have done it

more often

(stillness in motion)

what a fool   i am   when i am not

but

(o God)

if i am a fool

then let me be yours

let me be yours

[stands up]

good men will say

i have sinned   against you

i don't mind

they build churches   when forests exist

and trade on tuesdays   for sundays' sake

but i know

you know

(my beating heart)

how i suffer   our separation

[walks]

a lovesick suitor   i see your face

in a sparrow, in a stream

ever-present, out of reach

(Tantalus in Tartarus)

and when i turn away

i find you yet
            you delight   in the unseen places
      (God is also in the slime)
                                    for where else are you
                                          most needed?
    so do not make me wait
                      let me be where you are
                            there is no place for me
                                          here
    an exile in a foreign land
                amid customs   he can't understand
      (a deaf dog)
                            longing for a home
                                  he only remembers
                                          in a dream
                  o let me sleep   to wake
                                          no more
                                    [stops]
  and yet
                    does not this world
      (bone-white and cratered)
                            wax more lovely
                                          as it wanes?
    a path a post   the night, itself
                                  familiar and enduring
                  are they not more precious   in their passing?
                                    [goes on]
  never again   will i step outside   or
                            walk upright   or
        taste the insubstantial air
      (the moons of a mayfly)
  the stars will burn   and summer fade   and winter thaw

but not for me
time will f l o w
(the silent flood)
and cover/over every vestige
of having been
(everywhere, an unmarked grave)
i am content
the nocturne's allure   appears as it dis a p p e a r   s
one note dies   for another
to arise
to hold one's breath   is to lose one's life
(unless a grain of wheat)
so why resist?
if silence
is the word of God   then
He speaks   when i do not
so fill my throat with emptiness
and plug my lungs with prayer:
the one
the flower mutely mouths   in quiet longing
for the sun
[enters Auvers]
i arrive   to depart
and so arrive again
five hundred times:
this lamp, that bench
(have i noticed them before?)
i see them   for the last time   for the first time
the old   becomes the new
in the vivid light   of my fading gaze
(time, a ray)
here there is beauty!   there there is grace!

but the town is sleep
        and there is none but i   awake
          shall i rouse them from their beds and
    raise alarm against
               the all-infringing night?
   (the water, the well!)
but what sign would speak of the coming calamity?
     if i point: a tree
             if i call: the wind
  they cannot see   what has always been
               and so
         they think me mad
there is a fever
             [drops of blood]
   whose distemper shows   in sight unfounded
  (a veiled face, the fractalating dawn)
  but sanity
    is not reserved   for those who see
             what is
  (the naked sun)
     only
        a different kind
          of madness
to make them see
       with dying eyes
         has been my restless aim
    but my brush
   has not the wit   to speak to those
        who will not hear
no saint am i
  (Lord knows)
     nor martyr blessed   nor virtue's paragon

i only sought   to wake them up
                                so i could have
                                                a friend
what ocean squall or
                    furtive trial or
                                    thought-descending gloom
            could not be borne
                            through shrouded night
                by hearts   that share
                                            a tomb?
    i could not fit in men's designs   nor
                spark a woman's love
                        a needless speck   a blundered stroke
                            where else   have i
                                        to go?
                                [looks up]

to you
    (o stars!)
                i dedicate
        what light   i have
                            to share
                                        it isn't much
                                it won't last long
                        and you may never know
                                                    – but

i will not die
                    with it inside
                    and it is mine
                                        to give
                                    so take my gift
                            such as it is
and i shall witness bear:

                              for one brief round
        (my starry night)

                                    i burned

                                          in your array

so goodnight, good night
                  godspeed   God be with you

                                    i'll not see you again

        there are no words   to hold my thanks

                                    i'll miss you

                                          most of all

    for you stayed true

                  when others turned   and my weak will

                              would bend

        i'm not ashamed

                        i couldn't read   your signs

              nor heed   your prophesies

    it was enough

    (i hope you know)

                        to dwell within   your gaze

  and if my love

            impose you aught   i have one

                                    last request

      should you find

      (once i am gone)

                        a man   like me

                                          alone

        then speak to him

              in soft, sweet tones

                                so he might bide

                                          the dark

  all my life

      the lights on high   have kept

their constant course
yet i have learnt   so little
from their company
how much time
would i need
to grasp the meaning
of their movement?
were i to live
ten-thousand years
i'd know not more
than i do
now

(a dull mirror)
so what cause to grieve
a few years' loss
when lifetimes
won't suffice?
why seek?   why strive?
why stand against?
[more blood]
we end
where we begin
the vespered air   a bit of bread
why are not these enough?
i could not sit
in calm repose   and bide away
the time – no
i've lived each day
in frenzied fear
of God's exacting brow
what had i done
with my poor gifts

are they still safe

in me?

dare i return   with them

intact

and restore them   now in full?

o awful weight!

to bear Him back   what He has given

me

and so i break

apart my heart   and bleed

my soul entire

so i might show

by empty hands

His loan was not

misspent

[Place de la Mairie]

what others deem a humble inn

i make   an undiscerning tomb

for when i pass   within its frame

the world i'll leave

behind

what folly

to mourn the loss

of what was

never mine

(an unwed widow)

i am ready

[opens door]

a single light

a dreary gloam

the keeper   waits for me

and in his watch

the frightened look   of one who sees

                                        a ghost

(a Danish battlement)

he is not much   wrong

                for i come

                      in such a questionable shape

what happened to you?

              lifting up   my plastered shirt

                  i have tried to kill myself

he turns

         a paler shade   of white

sweet Jesus. Louise! O Christ, what have you done?

                     you would think   the bullet

                        were in him

             it is my body

(a grave mechanical)

             i am free to do with it what i will

he stares   agape

        as my clothes   release

the rain   upon his floor

(a metronome)

                water's grace

      is that it seeks   the lowest

                     place

his wife appears

(a hidden well)

     her face

        the two confer

   a mask concerned

         urgent whispers in the dark

she gasps

stay here

he dons a coat

i will not leave

the door slams   shut

for i have some place to go

with timid step

she comes in   close

(a deer, half-turned)

and questions   with her eyes

don't be afraid

a stifled cry

the storm will soon be past

in the welter

of creation   Behemoth

has its   place

[the staircase]

the gallows' steps

are steep and high

they rise to cast

(a spinning wheel)

back down again

my guilt confirms

i'll not be spared

though i do not

know my crime

a garret or a gutter

above the earth

[this floating bier]

shall bring me

to my rest

no one can grieve

the loss of him

who leaves no space

behind

my legacy

(a vacant room)

a panoply   of half-constructed

memories

fragments of

a life, misused

a field of wheat

cafés at night

flowers in a vase   these

simple sights

accuse me   now

as unimportant things

and yet

they're all i have

to show   i lived

the rest   is lost

in time

(that grey ocean)

i don't recall   what moved

my brush   to limn each

separate scene   nor

can i claim   some arch intent

that justified   the strain

could i have tread

some other path   then

i would have

turned aside   – but

i can affirm   that when

i worked   i could

forget   the pain

for from this world   so full

<pre>
                                        of woe
                    i've found   just three ways
                                                                              out
                                          the first is   drink
              that gilded door
          (so close at hand)
                                              to grim eternity
      a woman's touch
                              is second best
                                    were it not   so dearly
                                          bought
          only   the third
                              provides respite without
                                          a cost   deferred
                          and so i tried   to flee
                                                  myself
                                  in the pursuit
      he's upstairs
                                                                      of art
                      now were a man   to carve
                                  a cave
                          of wondrous delights
          (the staircase groans)
                                                  the door
      to which   was so concealed
                              that none   could enter in
          and no one glimpsed
                              the treasures there   or saw
          (a cautious knock)
                                              the wealth within
      and no one knew
                                  that door   or
</pre>

cave   or

man

it's me

had ever been

then would not   the world

(an open door)

be just the same   as though

he never   lived?

let me examine you

we like to think

virtue persists

when it   is not

observed ·

the bullet is still inside

and people love

i put it there

to hear of   him

who acts

without reward

there is a chance

everyone is glad   to know

that such   a man

exists

I can save you

but who would choose   to live

then i will do it again

as one

condemned to be

so good?

and why don't those

let me clean the wound

who swear   they would

as you like

seek out

those hidden

caves?

(echoes in the dark)

God consoles

the lonely   man

when others

look away

take this

He speaks

to him

i feel no pain

in measured beats

his pulse

a staunch   refrain

take it anyway

one cannot reason

with a corpse   or

[drinks]

a doctor

(bitter almonds)

our lives

are short   and

torturous

<<my father's study>>

little miracles

why did you come?

of misery

what a question

we hope   the days ahead

<<dust motes in a shaft of light>>

                                        hold better things
                                                in store
        (a golden glow)
                                but what
                will be
                        is all
            that's been
        <<a large book with leather binding>>
                                        time does not move
            (the room dissolves)
                            it does not move
                                                        at all
    <<i smell the pages
            gilded edges   the scent of glue   and gravity
                                                bare knees
                                        tucked close   i riffle
                    through the onionskin
            the solemn sway   of the grandfather clock
anna   rushes in   i look up
                    she giggles and points   to the far   corner
                        my cell   in saint-rémy
        paintings stacked   against the wall
                i turn back to her   an empty hall
                        wind whistles through the   trees
                                                i pull my beard
                            the frozen floor   my head
            begins to swim   the   shadows move
        there is no roof   crows   circle overhead
i hear my name
            paul   sits   in a chair   yellow
                            paper on th e walls
                                        he holds a   box

              he looks unwell
    i know   what is inside
            have i disappointed?   he shakes and speaks
  of Go d
       the floor rolls   he is deaf in his
  sincerity   blood trickles from t he box   i feel
                       sick
              and close my eyes
a row of lights   the rive r
       Seine   wicker chairs
  glasses twin kle in   the   night   people
        dressed in suits an d   sleeves   i look
                 at them
            no o   ne sees   m e
   they smile a nd speak in plea sant tone s
             i pour a drink   there
 is noth ing   l eft   an awful thir s t
            the p eople   laugh
   n o   faces
    my he art grows fa int   my veins run
                 d ry
a man a ppears   h e looks   like m e
       i a m afrai d
          he off ers m e a
  crys tal phial m y   thirs t   comm an ds
      i dr ink   it   d own
 he ta ke s   m y h a n d
          we st art to r is e
     the sk y   un f ur l s
   t he eart h is s ma ll
       it floats u pon an end l ess   sea
 the pe ople there are b orn to   d ie

everyth i n g   must com e to   na ug h t

i l o ok awa y

t he hollow ni g ht

a   canvas pain ted b l a ck

m y l u n gs breathe   o ut

the v o i d pour s   i n

dar k n e s s   all   aro un d

h e dro ps   my   h a nd

i sit   u p str aig ht

a ga rd e n ful l of fl o we rs

s ky afla m e   in   br ill iant   h u e s

st ately t r e e

m os sy t ur f

fig u re s   p a ss th roug hout   the g rou nd s

a pr oce ssion o f m e m or y

eve ry a c ti o n, e ver y wor d

a ll m y fo rm er   se lv es

pr e s e nt a nd   dis pla yed

i s ee it n o w

i s tar t t o   c ry

wh at hav e   i do ne ?

i c ann ot t urn   a wa y

fo r gi ve m e

f orgi v e m e

i f on ly   i ha d kn ow n

my o th e r s el f

for g iv e m e pl ea se

ca n   i   r etu r n?

plea se l et m e go

t he p a i n, th e pa i n

it t w is t s   t h e mi n d

it b lin d s t he   s o ul

i se e   i t n o w

                              c an i g o   b ac k ?

      i   ca n ' t g o   o n

                                    le t m e   r e tu rn

          i wo u l d s o li k e to   g o

              i   w o n't   f org e t

      i wo   n' t f o r   ge t

          th i s t im   e i s w e   ar

                              i w o n't   f o r   g   et

t he ma n is n ow   a wa sh with l i g ht

                    h e giv e s no si gn   o f a r e s   po n se

      i f e e l a wa r m th s p re a d   t hro u g h   m y li   m b s h is e y e s   s hi n in   g b r i ght

              m y min   d i s c a   l m

  m y b o d y   w ho l   e

                      i a m s o   f   u l l o f l   o ve

      t h   e g ar d e n   f   ad   es

              th   e m a n   l o   o k s   o n

    t hi s i s   w h a t   i   w a n t e d

>>

About the Author

Orion Taraban, Psy.D., is a clinical psychologist in private practice. His YouTube channel (@PsycHacks) has nearly 1 million subscribers and 200 million views, and his many media appearances have established him as a thought leader in popular psychology. He is also the best-selling author of *The Value of Others*, which examines his model of intersexual relationship dynamics. Though much of this book was written in Tokyo, Dr. Taraban currently lives in Napa, California.